Dear Parents:

D0199172

Congratulations! Your child is taking the first steps on an exciting journey. The destination? Independent reading!

STEP INTO READING® will help your child get there. The program offers five steps to reading success. Each step includes fun stories and colorful art or photographs. In addition to original fiction and books with favorite characters, there are Step into Reading Non-Fiction Readers, Phonics Readers and Boxed Sets, Sticker Readers, and Comic Readers—a complete literacy program with something to interest every child.

Learning to Read, Step by Step!

Ready to Read   Preschool–Kindergarten
• big type and easy words • rhyme and rhythm • picture clues
For children who know the alphabet and are eager to begin reading.

Reading with Help   Preschool–Grade 1
• basic vocabulary • short sentences • simple stories
For children who recognize familiar words and sound out new words with help.

Reading on Your Own   Grades 1–3
• engaging characters • easy-to-follow plots • popular topics
For children who are ready to read on their own.

Reading Paragraphs   Grades 2–3
• challenging vocabulary • short paragraphs • exciting stories
For newly independent readers who read simple sentences with confidence.

Ready for Chapters   Grades 2–4
• chapters • longer paragraphs • full-color art
For children who want to take the plunge into chapter books but still like colorful pictures.

STEP INTO READING® is designed to give every child a successful reading experience. The grade levels are only guides; children will progress through the steps at their own speed, developing confidence in their reading. The F&P Text Level on the back cover serves as another tool to help you choose the right book for your child.

Remember, a lifetime love of reading starts with a single step!

NO LONGER PROPERTY OF Anythink Libraries Rangeview Library District

For kids with loose teeth
—J.M.

Text copyright © 2016 by Julianne Moore
Cover art and interior illustrations copyright © 2016 by LeUyen Pham

All rights reserved. Published in the United States by Random House Children's Books,
a division of Penguin Random House LLC, New York.

Step into Reading, Random House, and the Random House colophon
are registered trademarks of Penguin Random House LLC.

Visit us on the Web!
StepIntoReading.com
randomhousekids.com

Educators and librarians, for a variety of teaching tools, visit us at RHTeachersLibrarians.com

Library of Congress Cataloging-in-Publication Data
Moore, Julianne.
Freckleface Strawberry : loose tooth! / by Julianne Moore ; illustrated by LeUyen Pham.
pages cm. — (Step into reading. Step 2)
Summary: Freckleface Strawberry wants very much for her first loose tooth to come out while
she is at school.
ISBN 978-0-385-39198-6 (hc) — ISBN 978-0-375-97368-0 (glb) — ISBN 978-0-385-39197-9 (pb) —
ISBN 978-0-385-39199-3 (ebk)
[1. Teeth—Fiction. 2. Schools—Fiction.] I. Pham, LeUyen, illustrator. II. Title.
III. Title: Loose tooth!.
PZ7.M78635Frn 2016
[E]—dc23
2015001796

Printed in the United States of America

10 9 8 7 6 5 4 3 2 1

This book has been officially leveled by using the F&P Text Level Gradient™ Leveling System.

Random House Children's Books supports the First Amendment and celebrates the right to read.

FRECKLEFACE STRAWBERRY
Loose Tooth!

by Julianne Moore
illustrated by LeUyen Pham

Random House 🏠 New York

Chapter 1

Freckleface Strawberry had
a loose tooth.

It was her first loose tooth.
It was in the front of
her mouth.

It was very, very loose.
She wanted to lose
the tooth soon.

She did not want to lose it
in her room.

She did not want to
lose it in the kitchen.

She did not want to lose it
on the playground.

She DID want to lose it
at school.

Chapter 2

At school,
all the kids would see.
At school,
she could go to the nurse.

At school,
the nurse would give her
a tiny tooth necklace
to wear around her neck.
The necklace was NICE.

Winnie had a necklace.

Windy Pants Patrick
had a necklace.

Noah had a necklace.

Freckleface Strawberry
did not have a necklace.

Chapter 3

Freckleface Strawberry
wiggled her tooth.
She wiggled her tooth
in the classroom.

She wiggled her tooth
in the lunchroom.

She wiggled her tooth
on the jungle gym.

"Freckleface Strawberry,"
said her teacher.
"You are not holding on
with both hands.
Please take your fingers
out of your mouth."

Windy Pants Patrick said,
"I told you so."

Chapter 4

Freckleface Strawberry
was worried
that she would not get
a tooth necklace.

The day was almost over
and her tooth
had not fallen out.

If she lost her tooth at home,
her mom would not
have a tooth necklace.

Her dad would not
have a tooth necklace.

Her sister had
a tooth necklace,
but she would not
give it to Freckleface.

Freckleface wanted
the necklace.
What could she do?

She was going to have
to do something.
She was going to have
to pull the tooth.
She was going to have
to pull HARD.

"Hey," said Windy Pants.
"Your tooth just fell out!
You should go to
the nurse."

And that is how Freckleface Strawberry got her tooth necklace.